AUTHOR'S NOTE

"Tall oaks from little acorns grow" (David Everett)

There are many different kinds of oak trees growing in Europe and North America, some as old as eight hundred years, but they all have one thing in common, that they all started life as a tiny acorn.

A mature oak tree will produce tens of thousands of acorns but only a very small number will ever grow into a tree. As an acorn it will need to escape being eaten by woodland creatures such as mice, squirrels, birds or insects. It needs to have a safe, dark place where it can lie undisturbed until germination. It also needs enough space where it can grow with enough food, light and water. As it grows into a mature tree it will have to escape the dangers of disease, of drought and storm and last but not least it will have to survive being chopped down by man. Many oak trees are cleared to make use of their valuable timber, for building ships, houses, furniture and fuel. They are also cleared to make way for roads or airports, as well as houses.

Where *The Acorn's Story* began

I have always been fortunate enough to live within easy access to woodland areas and have found great inspiration from walking in the countryside and observing nature. To work on *The Acorn's Story* I made frequent visits to the nearby National Trust estates at Tatton Park and Dunham Massey; these provided me with invaluable reference material in the shape of mature tree specimens, ancient hollow trees, deer, horses, and of course acorns! The lanes and pathways around my house as well as the more extensive natural beauty sites at Cannock Chase and Delamere Forest gave me a wealth of ideas and further inspiration. I made many trips to these sites and studied oak trees in all sorts of weather conditions in each of the four seasons. I shot numerous rolls of film to supply suitable reference material on which to base my drawings and also collected anything small enough to transport back to my studio including a very obliging frog! I grew small oak saplings from acorns which had just started to grow shoots; in short, I lived, worked and dreamed oak trees for the two years I was involved in the making of the book. Even now I am still learning about and marvelling at these most beautiful creations.

The
Acorn's Story

HAPPY CAT BOOKS

Published by Happy Cat Books Ltd.
Bradfield, Essex CO11 2UT, UK

This edition published 2003
1 3 5 7 9 10 8 6 4 2

A CIP catalogue record for this book is available from the British Library

ISBN 1 903285 48 8 Paperback

ISBN 1 903285 47 X Hardback

Printed in Poland

The Acorn's Story

Valerie Greeley

Happy Cat Books

Who shook me free?
"*I,*" said the breeze,
"*As I rustled the trees.*
I shook you free."

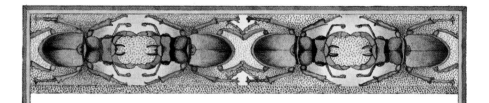

Who tilled the soil?
"*We,*" said the pigs,
"*As we searched under twigs.
We tilled the soil.*"

Who helped me root?
"*I,*" said the rain,
"*And it wasn't in vain.
I helped you root.*"

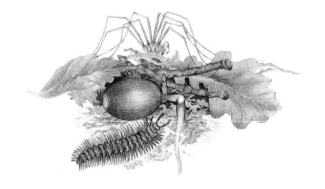

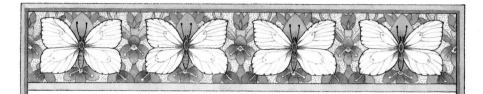

Who made me green?
"*I,*" said the light,
"*When the sun shone bright.*
I made you green."

Who watched me grow?
"I," said the mouse,
"From my cosy house.
I watched you grow."

Who made me strong?
"I," said the earth,
"I broadened your girth.
I made you strong."

Who made me change?
"We," said the seasons,
"We each had our reasons.
We made you change."

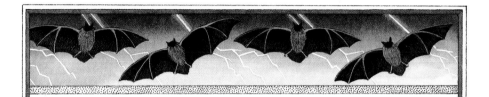

Who broke my bough?
"*I,*" said the lightning,
"*My power is frightening.
I broke your bough.*"

Who heard me cry?
"*I,*" said the owl,
"*As I watched the fox prowl.*
I heard you cry."

Who'll tell my story?
"I," said your seed,
"For the whole world to read.
I'll tell your story."

A GUIDE TO THE ILLUSTRATIONS

"Who shook me free?"

Acorns start life growing out of tiny flowers produced on the tree in spring. By the end of summer these acorns will be fully formed and will be loosened from their tiny cups by the wind.

An acorn falling under a large oak tree will stand little chance of survival as the parent will take all the food and light; the tree needs to spread its acorns to new places. This is where animals can help. Many animals such as mice and deer live beneath the shelter of the oak tree. This shelter can help protect them from danger and the acorns supply them with plenty of food to eat in the winter. Some animals such as mice and squirrels, and birds like jays, like to carry off the acorns and hide them until winter. This can help the tree to find new places to grow as often the animals forget to dig up all the acorns they have buried!

"Who tilled the soil?"

Like most seeds the acorn likes to be buried under the soil where it can stay safely in the dark until it germinates. It also finds it easier to take root if the ground is not too hard. Grazing animals help by treading the acorns under twigs and leaves and loosening the soil.

In the past, people who lived in the woods kept pigs. They used to let the pigs forage for food under oak trees as acorns made a tasty meal for free! The pigs would till the soil by shifting the leaves and earth with their feet and noses, this helped some acorns to root.

Many insects live on the forest floor and feed on the rotting leaves and the acorns. When an acorn rots it releases its food supply back to the earth where it feeds new plants and creepy crawlies such as worms, stag beetles, etc.

"Who helped me root?"

Just like frogs and snails, the acorn needs water. In order for the new root to grow, the soil must be moist and this moisture comes from the rain. The bigger the new tree grows the more water it will need. A mature tree can take up to 227 litres (50 gallons) of water a day through its roots! As well as water, the roots will also take nutrients from the soil so the plant can turn this into food.

The acorn first starts to grow a small root. This will grow into the ground, the bigger the tree the longer the root. It will also divide and spread sideways, this will eventually grow into a giant root system and will spread deep underground. As well as helping to get water and food these roots help anchor the tree into the ground and stop the tree blowing over.

Just above the tiny new root the acorn also grows a new shoot, this grows upwards into the light and will eventually grow into a stem with leaves. As the plant gets bigger it will grow branches and a thick trunk.

"Who made me green?"

New leaves start to appear in the springtime. At first the leaves are tiny, these tiny leaves allow plenty of light to get through to the forest floor. This is the time of the year when new spring flowers can be seen and the first butterflies like the yellow brimstone.

The sun is vital to the oak tree, as with all plants it needs the sun's rays to shine on to the green part of the leaf. The sun helps the plant to make food by a process called photosynthesis. Without the sun, the tree would die.

When the tree is young and the shoots are tender they are easily damaged by grazing animals like rabbits and deer. Unless the young tree has protection from these animals it will stand little chance of survival. Prickly plants such as hawthorn and holly can act as a barrier to these creatures.

"Who watched me grow?"

As the tree grows taller many creatures will make their homes in the branches. We all know that birds make their nests in the tree canopy but animals such as bats and squirrels also like to live high up in the tree. Mice prefer little nooks and crannies that develop in the trunk of the tree. The trunk is covered with bark that protects the tree - this bark often houses tiny insects that birds and bats like to eat. Lower down the tree, other animals such as badgers and foxes dig out their homes around the roots.

Many climbing plants like honeysuckle and ivy will use the trunk as a support and these in turn will provide good homes to small mice and birds. Moths such as the elephant hawk moth will be attracted to the nectar on the climbing plants. Caterpillars and larvae feeding on the leaves will, in turn, be eaten by the birds, nesting high in the branches of the oak tree.

"Who made me strong?"

A mature oak tree is a majestic sight. It can reach 30 metres in height and its canopy can spread as much as 40 metres. Each year it will grow a new layer, these layers make a ring pattern across the middle of the trunk. If you could cut through a trunk and count the rings you would have a good idea of the age of the tree.

In the summer the tree is in full leaf, but as the season changes into autumn these green leaves start to change to brown and will evenually fall off the tree. Thousands of leaves will fall before winter making a thick leaf carpet on the forest floor.

"Who made me change?"

As the nights grow longer and the days grow shorter, winter sets in. The temperature drops and the tree stands bare. We can see clearly all the many branches of the tree now that the leaves have fallen. If it is cold enough for snow, the tree can withstand the weight of the snowfall without its leaves. If these were still on the tree the branches would not be strong enough to cope and would break off.

Some creatures still find shelter around the tree even in the dark cold days of winter. The hedgehog curls up under the fallen leaves where it will hibernate until spring.

"Who broke my bough?"
In the course of its lifetime the oak tree will have to endure extremes of weather. It is very likely that at some stage it will be struck by lightning. Lightning can severely damage a tree but it usually manages to survive; whole boughs can break off but the rest of the tree will carry on growing.

Severe drought is much more damaging to a tree and can prove fatal.

"Who heard me cry?"
As the tree gets older its trunk gets thicker. A very old oak tree will have a thick hollow trunk and shorter stubby branches. The tree starts to die from the inside although the outer parts can carry on growing. These old hollow trees make excellent homes for all kinds of creatures. Barn owls, bats, foxes, all like to make their homes in the shelter of the old tree trunk.

The best time to see these creatures is night time. Many small insects like moths fly at night, so creatures who eat these such as bats, also come out when it's dark. Many small furry animals such as mice, shrews and voles are active at night and so it follows that birds like owls are also creatures of the night.

"Who will tell my story?"
Like all living things an oak tree will eventually die. Fortunately it makes so many acorns when it is alive to ensure that the species survives, with a little help from the squirrels!